FINDLAY:

A CINCINNATI PIG TALE

CURTIS SCRIBNER · ASHLEY SCRIBNER

ISBN: 0615741460

ISBN 13: 9780615741468

For Auggie

POP!

SMACK!

SPLASH!

Findlay rolled in the mud with his friend Crosley on a farm in Ohio. Rolling in the mud was fun, but Findlay wanted to do something new.

Findlay dreamed of a place where pigs could do whatever they wanted. They could shop, eat, explore and even find some more pig friends. That would be hog heaven!

Then, one day, Findlay heard Farmer Carl tell Farmer Pete, "Yep, I'm going to PORKOPOLIS on Sunday to bring some corn and beans to the market."

"PORKOPOLIS!

This must be the magical place of my dreams!" thought Findlay. He came up with a plan. He would sneak on Farmer Carl's truck when Farmer Carl brought his corn and beans to the market. He wanted to see

PORKOPOLIS!

The next morning Findlay
snuck onto Farmer Carl's
truck and was on his way.

OHIO

Before he knew it, Findlay was in PORKOPOLIS. He was happier than a pig at lunch!

Findlay opened up his city map and began to look for some pig friends.

He went to a "pig skin" game.

He heard lots of cheers but

WHERE WERE THE PIGS?

Findlay walked by the Ohio River
and saw a PURPLE BRIDGE!
He thought the bridge was lovely
and wanted to see it closer . . .

So he went sailing on the Ohio River but WHERE WERE THE PIGS?

"I'm sailing. Weeee! Weeee!"

Findlay walked into the city.
A whole bunch of joggers came
running towards him. Findlay
waddled as fast as he could
to avoid the joggers but didn't see
any swine. WHERE WERE THE PIGS?

A quick shower in a beautiful fountain gave Findlay time to cool off and relax after the race.

"OH LOOK! It's the three little pigs," snorted Findlay! Findlay huffed and puffed to get the pigs' attention, but they didn't move. After looking at the pigs' different and bright colors, Findlay realized they were statues and continued on his journey.

All of this walking was going to make Findlay the skinniest pig ever! Findlay took a break at a train station. He thought, "WHERE WERE THE PIGS?"

Next Findlay saw an art museum!
"I bet they have some Warhogs
or Pigcassos," said Findlay,
"but WHERE WERE THE PIGS?"

Findlay climbed a really big hill. He was as *hot* as a *barbeque* and sure could use some ice cream!

Findlay stumbled upon a pretty street. There was an ice cream store on the street! After hogging down some ice cream, Findlay realized it was getting late.

Hyde Pork's Greatest Ice Cream

Black Rasp"boar"y Chocolate Chip!

Time sure does fly when you're having fun! Findlay had to get back to the market and Farmer Carl's truck! He still wondered WHERE WERE THE PIGS?

Findlay rode a city bus
back to the market.

NOW LEAVING
PORKOPOLIS
COME BACK SOON!

Findlay snuck onto Farmer Carl's truck and headed home. Findlay saw the city in the distance. He thought about how much fun he had on his trip.

NOW LEAVING

PORKOPOLIS

COME BACK SOON!

Findlay watched an exciting pigskin game, saw a beautiful purple bridge and sailed on a boat.

He raced with joggers, showered
in a fountain and stumbled upon
a wonderful train station.

He visited an art museum, climbed up a big hill and shopped at some stores.

PORKOPOLIS might not have any pigs, but Findlay still had a fun adventure!

Findlay jumped off of Farmer Carl's truck. Crosley was waiting for him. Findlay had a great idea. He was going to sneak back to PORKOPOLIS.

Next time he was going to bring his best friend Crosley with him! PORKOPOLIS will be even more fun with Crosley!

Watch out Cincinnati,

HERE COME THE PIGS!!

Thanks to Cincinnati, "Porkopolis,"
a great place to live.

Special *thanks* to our parents, Hyde
Park United Methodist Church,
Mandy Gilmore, Kathy O'Malley,
Keith Prenger and ArtWorks.

Ashley and Curtis Scribner grew up on opposite sides of Ohio and met at Xavier University. Ashley, an artist, and Curtis, an avid reader and lover of literature, always knew *they* would make a great team for a children's book. They got married, moved to New York City, travelled the world, but, all the while, their hearts remained in Cincinnati. Ashley and Curtis now live back home in "PORKOPOLIS," and work as an art teacher and corporate attorney. They spend their free time creating and spending time with their baby Augustus Xavier and faithful dog Scully.

Made in the USA
Middletown, DE
18 October 2016